The
Summertime
SANTA

Books by the same author

Freddie and the Enormouse

For older readers

Something Watching
The Camera Obscura
The Haunted Sand
The Plant that Ate the World
The Shaman's Stone
Why Weeps the Brogan?

The
Summertime
SANTA

Hugh Scott

Illustrations by
John Rogan

WALKER BOOKS
LONDON

To Samantha,
for her enthusiasm

First published 1990 by Walker Books Ltd
87 Vauxhall Walk, London SE11 5HJ

Text © 1990 Hugh Scott
Illustrations © 1990 John Rogan

First printed 1990
Printed and bound in Great Britain by
Richard Clay Ltd, Bungay, Suffolk

British Library Cataloguing in Publication Data
Scott, Hugh
The summertime santa.
I. Title
823'.914 [F]
ISBN 0-7445-1538-6
ISBN 0-7445-1725-7 Pbk

CONTENTS

THE
EMPTY BOXES

"Boxes are very empty today," said Caireen to herself.

She felt inside her oldest, most favourite shoe box, scratching into each corner, but she found only fluff and pencil sharpenings.

She said, "Oh, dear," and rubbed the fluff from her fingers onto her skirt. "Where *is* my plastic teapot? Were *are* my pens? And my padlock that won't open, and —"

Caireen pressed the end of her matchbox, smiling, because she *knew* that in the matchbox was her most favourite treasure. The inside of the matchbox popped out onto the carpet.

Caireen's favourite object was *not* in the matchbox.

"What *is wrong* today?" said Caireen.

She searched the carpet to be *quite* sure, but she really *was* sure that nothing had jumped out when the box dropped.

She left the matchbox in two pieces and walked round her bed in her stocking feet. She knelt on the carpet and peered under the bed.

Caireen saw enough fluff to fill all the space in her shoe box. She saw – well, she saw all the things *you* see when you look under *your* bed. And she saw her most favourite box of all – Grandad's pencil case.

Grandad's pencil case was a plain, beautiful, wooden box, long enough to hold a pencil, and deep enough to hold three pencils, and wide enough to hold *fifteen* pencils. Well, twelve pencils.

And it was packed with pencils. Caireen knew it was packed with pencils, because she used the box *every day* – except today, of course. And she hadn't used it yesterday because her drawing book was full. And she hadn't used it the day before, because she couldn't be bothered drawing. (And her drawing book was full.)

Caireen pulled the box from under a wellington and rubbed dust from its top. The top had a groove in it, to let Caireen's thumbnail catch hold, so she could slide the lid off and let her fingers in to rummage among the pencils. The box looked like this:

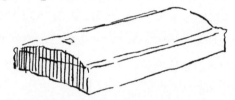

Or if she opened it, like this:

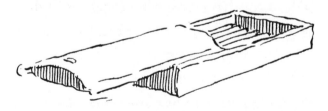

At least, it *should* have looked like that. But when Caireen's thumbnail caught the groove and slid the lid back, her mouth let out a gasp.

Her eyes made a few tears – which Caireen decided she would keep for later.

When Caireen opened her
pencil case, it looked like this:
EMPTY!
Caireen couldn't believe it!
She sat back *bump!* on the carpet.
She stared hard into her pencil case,
as if staring could bring back her pencils.
Why, these had been Grandad's pencils!
Some of them were so old-fashioned that they
had never been painted. They were made of
plain wood! Some had never been sharpened
and were beautifully flat at both ends. These,
of course, were the ones Caireen would never
use. She kept them as special treasures – more
special than the treasure in her matchbox – or
rather, not in her matchbox. That was only
an old rubber after all, and so dry it made
marks on her drawings. Though it was a
lovely doughy shape.
But where were her pencils?
That was a puzzle.
In fact, it was more than a puzzle.
It was a little bit frightening.

COUNTING UNTIL CHRISTMAS

Caireen had no brother or sister to blame for the missing pencils, so she had to think.

She thought.

She said to her pencil case, "You were *full* of pencils last time I used you. Not yesterday. Not the day before. Last week? Not last week. Surely not *last month*?"

Caireen searched the top drawer of her chest of drawers and found her drawing book.

She opened it at the last page. She remembered doing the drawing. She looked at the date. (Caireen always wrote the date on her drawings because famous artists did this, and she wanted to be famous.)

"Well!" she told the pencil case, as it lay listening on the carpet. "It *was* last month that I used the pencils!"

She examined her drawing. She remembered spending all morning at her bedroom window sitting high on her chest of drawers, her feet on the back of a chair, the drawing book on her knees, watching a removal van parked next door, and drawing the men carrying furniture.

And things.

Some very odd things.

Caireen frowned as she thought.

She remembered two men carrying *very large* boxes with the word TOYS printed on them.

She had seen one removal man dragging a *huge* sack overflowing with what looked like empty Christmas stockings.

And that was last month. August. Now it was September. But surely Christmas was ages away? And surely the people moving in next door couldn't be filling *quite* so many stockings for their children, when Christmas did come?

Caireen counted the months on her fingers, saying, "September" to her thumb.

Saying "October" to her forefinger.

Saying "November" to her middle finger, and "December" to her third finger.

Her pinkie felt lonely at not being counted, so she counted again starting with her pinkie, calling *it* "September" – but when she had counted again, Christmas was still nearly four months away.

Why would her new neighbours have Christmas stockings so soon after summer?

And where were Caireen's pencils?

And where was her rubber out of the matchbox?

And why was her favourite shoe box so empty?

Caireen wanted to know.

She decided to speak to Edward.

IT'S VERY PUZZLE-MAKING

Caireen pulled on her shoes, trundled downstairs and told her mum she was visiting Edward. Mum wanted to know where the new tennis balls were, and waved an empty tennis-ball box at Caireen.

Then Caireen ran beneath the September sun, along the drive, dashed across the lawn, trotted round the tennis court that Daddy had built, crawled through the branchy gap in the hedge, darted across Edward's lawn, swung twice on the rope that hung from their Tarzan tree, clattered up the stone path and pushed open the back door to Edward's house.

"Edward!" called Caireen.

Her voice rushed through Edward's house. It didn't find Edward downstairs in the lounge or in the dining room, or in the kitchen, or in the pantry, or in the study, or in the drawing room (beside the dining room) or hiding under the stairs in the dark cubby hole.

So it rushed up the stairs (Caireen's *voice* rushed up the stairs) but it didn't find him in the shower room, or in the bathroom, but it *did* find him in his bedroom, so it didn't go into any other rooms.

"Come up!" called Edward, when Caireen's voice reached him.

She went up.

Edward's toy cupboard was open and boxes lay on the carpet, with Edward sitting among them.

Caireen was surprised because she knew Edward was not a toy boy, but more interested in games and puzzles and books.

"Are you giving your toys away?" asked Caireen.

"I'm looking for something," said Edward.

"Looking for what?" asked Caireen.

"It's very puzzle-making," said Edward, who used words in his own way.

"What is puzzle-making?" asked Caireen. She was very patient with Edward. He never said *exactly* what he meant until you had asked him a heap of questions. But he was clever, and knew things Caireen didn't know.

"What," asked Caireen again, "is puzzle-making?"

"This box is puzzle-making," said Edward. He smiled up at Caireen and she wanted to pat Edward's hair because it was red and thick and springy. But she didn't.

He was pointing at a black plastic box.

"It was full of metal puzzles," said Edward. "Now it's empty. That's what I'm looking for."

"*My* boxes are empty," said Caireen. "Grandad's pencils have gone."

"I expect you left them out, and your mum put them somewhere."

"I expect," said Caireen, "you left your puzzles out, and *your* mum put them somewhere."

"I definitely left them in their box," said Edward.

He shut the box and opened it. He stared into it as if staring could bring back his puzzles, just as Caireen had stared into her pencil case.

"It is puzzle-making," said Edward again.

"Have you looked in your other boxes?" asked Caireen. She lifted a jigsaw puzzle box.

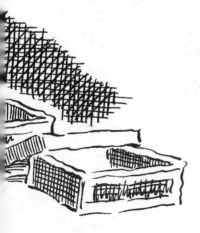

"They won't be in there," said Edward.

Caireen shook the box. "There's *nothing* in here," she said.

"You can hear the noise it's not making."

Edward snatched the jigsaw puzzle box, opened it, and tipped it up. But nothing fell out. He pushed his hand inside. He peered inside. He threw the box back among his toys. "It is rather empty," he agreed.

They looked in all Edward's boxes. His Monopoly box was empty. His chess box was empty. His Scrabble, Ludo and Cluedo boxes were empty.

The fact is – *every one was empty.*

Except for fluff in the corners, and half a tea biscuit in his chess box.

"I think," said Caireen, "it's something to do with my new neighbours."

To Caireen's surprise, Edward said, "So do I."

"You do?" said Caireen.

"Yes," said Edward. "I saw two of their children late last night, playing tennis on your tennis court."

"Late last night!" cried Caireen. "In the moonlight? I haven't seen any children! What did they look like? Oh! I've just thought!"

"What?"

"Mum's tennis-ball box was empty! Do you think these children could have stolen the tennis balls?"

"Well..."

"Our back door is always open," said Caireen, "and your back door is always open."

"Yes —"

"They could have sneaked into the house."

"Let's go and ask them," said Edward, and because this was sensible, Caireen agreed, and they left Edward's house, clattered on the stone path, darted across Edward's lawn to the Tarzan tree where they spent rather a long time swinging on the rope – crawled through the branchy gap in the hedge, ran across Caireen's lawn, trotted round the tennis court, crunched down the drive and out the gate to the road, walked on the pavement and stared up the next drive at the new neighbours' house.

TREES WATCHING

The new neighbours' house was just as big as Caireen's house – which was just as big as Edward's house. Caireen and Edward could not see the new neighbours' house very well, because the drive curved among rhododendron bushes and silver birch trees, two larch trees, a Christmas tree, a monkey-puzzle tree and others.

Caireen and Edward walked along the drive (among the trees) and went up four steps to the front porch. Edward pressed the door bell.

Caireen went down three of the steps because she was shy and wondered if it was right to ask people if they had stolen things.

But no one answered the door.

That was strange, because Edward agreed

with Caireen that *someone* was at home.

"Didn't you hear a hammer hammering?" said Edward.

"I heard a song singing," said Caireen, who liked to copy Edward's funny ways of talking, "and a knitting machine knitting, and other noises noising. But everything's silently quiet now and I think we should go home."

Edward pressed the bell again.

He looked down at Caireen (who was now standing on the gravelly drive).

"They don't want to answer," Edward told Caireen, "because they feel guilty. THEY FEEL GUILTY ABOUT PLAYING TENNIS ON YOUR TENNIS COURT."

"They'll hear you!" hissed Caireen, and she stared at the door hoping no one would rush out and shout at them.

No one rushed out and shouted angrily. No one stamped and waved their fists. No one turned red and glared, and threatened to tell Caireen's mother.

So that was all right.

Except that the house was quiet.

And the trees stood still, watching Caireen and Edward.

Edward came down three steps and said, "I THINK WE SHOULD GO HOME."

Caireen said, "Ssssh!"

"WE'RE GOING HOME NOW," said Edward, and he crunched on the gravelly drive beside Caireen, *crunch! crunch! crunch!* away from the front door, Edward glancing back at the windows, Caireen crunching quickly between the trees, ahead of Edward. Then she heard just her own feet crunching.

Edward? thought Caireen.

She turned.

Edward had gone.

WOOLLY RUBBISH

Caireen's mouth opened to say "Oh!" but before it could speak, one of the trees spoke.

It said, "*Come here!*"

Caireen stared at the house windows, and the windows stared back.

She saw no one looking out and dashed behind the tree. Edward was as flat as an Apache against the trunk.

"Why are you hiding?" asked Caireen.

"I want to see inside," said Edward.

"Inside the tree?"

"Inside the house. We'll go round the back and look in the windows."

"What for?"

"To find out about our empty boxes, of course."

"What if someone catches us?"

Edward frowned, and Caireen wanted (again) to pat his red curls. "We'll say we're looking for our ball," said Edward.

Caireen suddenly did not want to pat Edward's curls. "We can't tell lies," she told him.

"I thought your mum had lost her tennis balls?"

"Yes —"

"Then that's what we're looking for."

Caireen decided that Edward was right – though telling someone you are looking for your ball, usually means that you kicked it over the wall by mistake – not that you think your new neighbours have stolen it.

Caireen ran with Edward among rhododendrons, making sure that no one watched from the windows.

The garden at the back of the house had many trees and bushes around a large lawn, all still thick with summer leaves. Caireen and Edward sat among the bushes deciding which window to look in first.

"Someone may come out the back door," said Caireen, "to put rubbish in the bin."

"I think," said Edward, peering under rhododendron leaves, "that you're right." And he held the leaves aside so Caireen could see.

Caireen saw four dustbins. Their lids sat too high on top of heaped-up rubbish – bright colours of rubbish. "Well!" breathed Caireen. "Wool," she told herself. "Scraps of socks and wormy ends of wool."

Caireen thought of what was in *her* bins next door. Tins and packets and scrapings of food.

She was about to tell Edward that this rubbish was different, when the handle of the back door clicked and the door opened.

Down the back step came a bin bag with hands.

THE WRINKLY BOY

Caireen gasped and the rhododendron leaves rustled as she squirmed back.

"Look! Look!" she cried and Edward look-looked.

The bin bag went to the bins and sat down. A head appeared beside the bin bag, and the body that belonged to the head walked back to the house. It was as small as Caireen's little brother (if she had had a little brother) and as sturdy as a bush. Its legs wore jeans and its top was buried in a baggy jumper. The jumper, Caireen noticed, had coloured woolly worms clinging to the sleeve, and the jeans were fluffy with dust.

Before the body shut the door, it turned towards the fresh air and drew in a breath. It said, "Aaah!" The door shut and Caireen and Edward looked at each other with their mouths open.

"Oh, Edward!" whispered Caireen. "What a strange little boy!"

"A really wrinkly face," muttered Edward.

"And such a deep voice!" screeched Caireen (quietly).

"And very big hands," said Edward. "And there *was* somebody," said Edward some more, "to answer the door."

"Oh, yes," said Caireen.

"Now's our chance to look in the window." Edward crept across the lawn.

Caireen waited behind the rhododendron bush. She wondered what Mum would say about people who looked through other people's windows.

She knew that Granny would turn over in her grave.

Caireen ran, hoping nobody would tell Granny.

She stopped beside Edward, under the high windowsill.

"I can't see in," whispered Edward. "We need something to stand on." And he sneaked away leaving Caireen under the window.

Caireen was surprised at being left alone. Boys were so thoughtless! What if that strange child came out again? Or if his father appeared – like the person who hadn't come out the front door, red-faced and fists waving.

Caireen looked at the back door.

It was quite shut and seemed content to stay that way.

She looked up at the window, but it wasn't very interesting, so she looked at the trees around the lawn.

Caireen was quite sure the trees were watching.

She stared at the corner of the house where Edward had gone.

She looked back at the trees and decided they were closer. That yew – surely – had stepped right onto the grass, its long woody toes digging into the ground.

Oh, don't be silly, said Caireen to Caireen.

Then Edward came crunching, carrying a metal bucket.

Caireen said, "Ssssh!"

Edward said, "Ssssh!" and placed the bucket upside down under the window, and stood on it.

"Golly!" he said peering in. "Look at all those mugs! And plates! They're so small! With one mouldy sandwich and a dry scone each! And the chairs are so high around the table! And —"

Caireen pushed Edward making him step down, and she stepped up and stared at the mugs with holly printed round their rims and the plates with reindeer running round the edges, and —

Oops!

Inside the room, a door opened. Caireen ducked, then peeped, ducked again, said, "Oh!" peeped, stared, ducked, peeped and fell off the bucket.

"Careful!" whispered Edward and caught Caireen, helping her to step down.

"It's full of tiny strange children!" cried
Caireen (quietly).

"The bucket?" asked Edward.

"That room! With wrinkly faces and big
hands! Listen!"

They listened to a deep murmur of talk coming through the window, and Caireen crunched to the grass, not caring whether the trees were closer or not – oh! if only they *were* closer it wouldn't be so far to run! and she ran! ran! Edward at her side saying, "Don't run!" but he ran with her among the rhododendrons! Oh, dear! How strange and frightening!

"Oh, Edward!" gasped Caireen and held Edward's arm. "I want to go home! Please! Oh! Come! Come on —!"

"I hear something," said Edward. "Be quiet, Caireen."

Edward stood tall, peering through the leaves, and Caireen listened because Edward was listening. She heard a deep, sad murmur rolling across the sunlit lawn and drifting among the trees.

"The children are singing!" cried Caireen (not very quietly).

"I want to hear!" said Edward.

And this is what they heard:

Mmmmm! We are eating!
We are eating! Mmmmm!
We are eating slowly!
For the food is grimmmmm!

Oh, for the days of the Summertime Santa!
Oh, for the days of himmmmm!
Gone are the days of the Summertime Santa!
How we dream of himmmmm!

Mmmmm! We are singing!
We are singing! Mmmmm!
We are singing slowly!
For our song is grimmmmm!

Oh, for the days of the Summertime Santa!
Oh, for the days of himmmmm!
Gone are the days of the Summertime Santa!
How we dream of himmmmm!

Mmmmm! We are working!
We are working! Mmmmm!
We are working slowly!
For the work is grimmmmm!

Oh, for the days of the Summertime Santa!
Oh, for the days of himmmmm!
Gone are the days of the Summertime Santa!
How we dream of himmmmm!

When the voices sang of working, Caireen heard chairs moving.

Then the chorus faded and Caireen and Edward shared the silence with the trees.

"What do you make of that!" gasped Edward. "Children who sing like men! And a whole roomful of them!" Edward looked straight into Caireen's eyes. He told her, "I want to get inside that house!"

SCONE MIX

When Edward said he wanted into the neighbours' house, Caireen thought she would say, *But you can't!*

Then she thought she would say, *What would your mum say!*

Then she thought she would say, *What if they catch you!*

Then Edward said, "Stop opening and shutting your mouth like a goldfish! Come on!"

Edward dashed across the lawn.

He stopped at the door and turned the handle.

Caireen saw a dark slit as the door opened inwards.

Edward beckoned.

Caireen ran to him and whispered, "But you

can't! What would your mum say! What if they catch you!!"

Edward opened the door further and stepped inside.

Oh! Caireen's heart bobbed like a yo-yo! Wasn't Edward brave! Caireen knew, of course, that Edward was brave. Why, last summer when he was on holiday in Cornwall a dog had slipped over a cliff, tumbling terribly fast, yelping Help! Help! Everyone knew the dog would land on the rocks and the sea would come crashing in, then Edward —

But Caireen's heart was being a yo-yo. She stepped into the house behind Edward, because she did not want to be left alone with the trees.

When she stepped inside, her doubts about being in her neighbours' house vanished – because her foot shot away as if she had stood on a pencil.

It was a second before Caireen saw what had made her slip.

It was a pencil.

She picked it up.

She prodded the pencil against Edward's back. (He was opening another door.)

"It's from my pencil box!" whispered Caireen.

Edward smiled grimly. Caireen asked him to keep the pencil for her because her skirt had no pockets.

She stepped with him into the room where the strange children had sung.

The room was a kitchen. The chairs sat back from the table. Bread crumbs and scone crumbs dotted the little plates, and tea dregs cooled in the tiny mugs.

Edward lifted a scone crumb and tasted it. His nose wrinkled, and he put the crumb back on its plate.

He opened a cupboard. Which was empty. He opened other cupboards which were empty, except – Caireen noticed – for fingermarks, as if children had been feeling around for food.

A plastic sack on the floor, said:

> **SCONE MIX**
> *worst quality*

Edward frowned at this, and his red curls hung over his forehead.

Caireen looked away from Edward's curls, and noticed a cupboard high on the wall, with no fingermarks on its door. She put a chair under the cupboard and stood toe-tippy on the seat and pulled the door. Loaves were stacked inside.

A tag on one loaf said:

Best before 28th August

"And this is September," Caireen reminded herself.

All the tags said the same.

"Poor little things," thought Caireen. (She meant the children – not the tags.)

Edward's head had disappeared, because he was peering out of the kitchen door.

His hand waved at Caireen and she crept after him into a passage.

"I hear the knitting machine," breathed Caireen.

They stepped into the hall of the house where the front door let daylight through its glass panel.

The sound of the knitting machine came from a room across the hall.

Edward led Caireen to the door.

A floorboard creaked under Edward's heel.

The knitting machine whirred.

They listened at the keyhole.

Edward turned the handle.

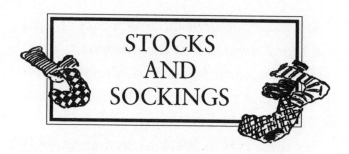

STOCKS
AND
SOCKINGS

Caireen saw socks and stockings. Stockings
and socks stacked high as the light bulbs and
trampled into soft paths for someone to walk
among the woolly mountains.

"It's a stock and socking factory!" gasped
Caireen.

But Edward frowned and lifted a stocking.
"It's old and darned!" he said.

"Ooh!" whispered Caireen. "It's not a
factory! These are the socks and stockings I
saw carried into the house from the removal
van!"

Edward pulled Caireen along the path, as
soft as walking on a bed.

The machine said *whirr whirr*.

Daylight bloomed bright through windows.
Whirr, whirr.

Around a coloured mountain they stepped,
and found a woman at the machine.

Her white curls bounced as she pushed
and pulled at the machine. Her tomato face
sagged with sadness.

Her dress was as black as soot in a
chimney.

A song squeezed from her sagging lips:

>"I _hate_ wearing black
>All down my back –
>If I _can't_ wear red
>I'd rather be ded —"

"She can't spell," whispered Caireen, but Edward shushed her, and they leaned against the mountain and listened.

>"I _wa-ant_ to bake
>A Chrissymass cake.
>And _dec_orate
>My husband's plate
>With _mist_letoe
>And oh! Oh! Oh!"

Sobs shook the woman's fat bits, and her sadness made Caireen want to pat her.

Edward pointed to sacks in a row beneath the window. Caireen read the words on one sack:

GNOMES' VESTS AND DRAWERS

She read the words on the next sack:

>_GNOMES' LONG STOCKINGS_
>_AND SCARVES_

She read the words on the sack beside the next sack:

GNOMES' WINTER TIGHTS

She read the words on the sack beside the sack beside the next sack:

GNOMES' HATS

She read the words on the sack beside the sack beside the sack beside the next sack:

GNOMES' WAISTCOATS
AND JERKINS

She read the words on the last sack:

GNOMES' COATS AND MITTENS

"Those clothes," whispered Edward, "are what she is making the socks and stockings into. But *why* is she using old socks and stockings? Gnomes' vests and drawers certainly are made of wool – *everybody* knows that! And their long stockings and scarves are made of wool."

"Everybody knows that," whispered
Caireen – who had never learned what
gnomes' underwear was made of.

"And their winter tights are made of
wool," continued Edward. "But their hats
should be made of *felt*. And their waistcoats
and jerkins should be made of *leather*. And
their coats and mittens should made of
sheepskin."

Caireen was very impressed that Edward
knew these things. "How do you know?" she
whispered.

"The same way," breathed Edward, "that
I know who that woman is! I've seen her in
Christmas card pictures – usually feeding the
reindeer, or lifting a sack from the sleigh.
Don't you recognize her? She's *only* Mrs
Santa Claus! Mother Christmas! Father
Christmas's wife!"

NORGOST
AND
VEGGLESTROM

Caireen stared at the woman (who had
stopped sobbing and was unravelling a sock
and winding the sock's wool onto her
machine).

Was Edward joking? Caireen knew that
Mrs Santa Claus ought to be fat like this
woman – but shouldn't she be jolly? And
dressed in red like her husband? And
honestly, Caireen wasn't sure that Mother
Christmas was *real* – because she wasn't sure
that *Father* Christmas was real.

Caireen tried to imagine the woman
smiling.

Why, yes. Those apple-bright cheeks *ought*
to be smiling.

And that dark-as-a-chimney dress *ought* to
be red.

And – Caireen was quite sure of this – the woman *ought* to be baking Chrissymas cake and mince pies!

Caireen decided to talk to Edward seriously. She took his hand and led him away from the bright windows among the woolly mountains.

She would take him into the garden where they wouldn't be disturbed. But as they approached the door of the stocking room, footsteps clumped through the hall.

So they trotted around a socky mountain to hide, and were so astonished at what they saw, that they hardly heard the door open. Whoever came through the door did not follow Caireen and Edward, but went grumbling towards the *whirr! whirr!* of the machine.

Which was lucky.

Because...

Staring at Caireen and Edward – just as Caireen and Edward were staring at *them* – were two wrinkly children.

The wrinkly children stood as tall as Caireen's elbow. Their jumper sleeves were cut short to fit their arms, and their jeans were folded up to fit their legs. Bent tennis rackets dangled in their strong hands.

"Oh!" whispered Caireen.

"Corks!" gasped Edward.

"Oooh!" yelped the wrinkly children and dived head-first into socky mountains, wriggling in until only their feet showed.

"Get them!" hissed Edward.

Caireen pulled one foot and Edward pulled another (on a different child).

The children slid from the mountains on their tummies, gaping round at Caireen and Edward.

One said in his deep voice, "Such a thig has never habbened before!"

The other said, "Oh, horribles! Horribles! Whad'll we do!" and he curled up, thick legs tight in his jeans, arms bulging in his old jumper – and wept.

"Sid up, Norgost," said the other child. "Sid up and be a gnome! These are not the derrible children Santa spoke of." He darted his fingers at Caireen and Edward. "Their faces be indelligent and kind."

Norgost stood up. He knuckled his eyes

with manly hands and blinked at Edward, then at Caireen.

"I think you are right, Vegglestrom," he said, "indelligent and kind. Berhaps they will not tell anyone they have seen us. It is most dreadful," said Norgost to Edward, "for a human child to see Santa's gnomes —"

"Are you really gnomes!" breathed Caireen.

"Ob course," said Norgost.

"You're very small," said Caireen as if, perhaps, she could help the gnomes grow bigger.

"We be not small!" whispered Norgost. "We be normal!" He frowned up at Caireen. "You be large, like all humans."

"Oh, no!" said Caireen. "I'm not large! My mum says —"

"Caireen!" said Edward, sounding like a school teacher. "Does it matter? These must be the children I saw in your tennis court. Look at their rackets. They aren't rackets at all. They're snow shoes. And didn't you hear what Norgost said?" Edward prodded

Caireen with a sharp finger. "He said, 'Santa's gnomes'. All these wrinkly children are Santa's gnomes."

"Wrinkly children!" cried Vegglestrom.

"*Santa's* gnomes?" said Caireen. "But they're dressed in rolled-up jeans and cut-up jumpers. *Santa's* gnomes wear felt hats and leather waistcoats and leather jerkins —"

"Be quiet," said Edward, and Caireen blinked, deciding she didn't like Edward's red curls after all.

"Please sit down," said Edward to Vegglestrom and Norgost.

His finger ordered Caireen to sit, so she sat on the wool-sock-soft floor.

"Tell us what's wrong," said Edward to the gnomes. "I recognized Mrs Santa Claus. She sang a sad song. She is turning all these mountains of socks and stockings into gnome clothes when she should be baking. And all you gnomes are eating only the worst food and wearing rolled-up jeans and cut-up jumpers."

"And," said Norgost, "we sing sad songs also."

"We heard you," said Caireen, remembering the singing in the kitchen. Could these strange children really be Santa's gnomes?

"Our troubles are great," sighed Vegglestrom.

"Great horribles," breathed Norgost.

"Do you know," said Vegglestrom, "how long Father Christmas has been giving toys to children? Neither do we. But he be fed up. Until summer he was OK. Jolly as ever. Then one day he trampled into the workshop at the North Pole, without letters in his hand.

He was sad as a reindeer wid no sleigh. 'No THANK YOU letters again this morning,' he sighs, and we all shake our heads and gontinue hammering and cutting and glueing and sewing and —"

"Ged on with it!" said Vegglestrom.

"Horribles, it was, to see Santa so sad. He kept hoping for letters. For six months he hoped, but – not one letter of THANK YOU. Ain't children derrible? After all the works we done, hammering and cutting and glueing and sewing and —"

"Thigs were never habby after that," said Vegglestrom. "As each day came without letters, Santa walked with his head bowed.

He changed his red clothes for black, and Mrs Claus also he made wear black. He grew afraid that he could not pay the bills so he switched off the heating." Vegglestrom shrugged. "You know how it is. When peoples is feeling down, they be scared the money will run out. And without heating, we could not work. Ice gathered on our clothes. I dropped my felt hat and it was so cold it broke into tiny-toaty pieces."

"Oh, no!" whispered Caireen.

"Things went from worse to bad," sighed Vegglestrom. "Everybody's clothes broke. Santa decided we should move to a place less cold. So we moved here. But we had not clothes, so packed in boxes marked TOYS we were, to keep us warm during the removal —"

"I saw those boxes!" said Caireen. "I told you, Edward! I saw them last month —!"

"Yes! Yes!" said Edward. "Please go on," he urged Vegglestrom.

"Vell," sighed Vegglestrom, so loudly that Caireen was sure that Mrs Claus and whoever was with her, would hear it above the *whirr whirr* of the knitting machine, "we had to st* $%."

"What did you say?" asked Edward.

Vegglestrom sighed again, and glanced sadly at Norgost.

Norgost sighed. "We had to steal," he told Edward.

A tear balanced in his eye then ran down the wrinkles in his cheek. "You, Vegglestrom, tell these kind and indelligent children," he wept.

"We had to steal. Socks and stockings were easy for us to find, knowing that children keep them on their carpets until it is time to hang them up for Christmas." Vegglestrom waved at the heaps of socks and stockings. "Mother Christmas – that is, Mrs Santa Claus – is making them into proper clothes for us, though —"

"Tell them the rest," moaned Norgost, "and save the worst for last."

"We could not make toys no longer. We had nothing to make them out of. All we had was our store of boxes. We always have more boxes than we need, because we never know how many childrens will want toys at the next Christmas."

"But you had no toys to put in the boxes!" guessed Edward.

"That is it," said Vegglestrom. "No toys to put in them. Nod one doy. Nod vun zingle doy."

"So you stole our toys!" Caireen stood straight. "From our boxes! That is terrible!"

"Derrible!" agreed Vegglestrom.

"Horribles," agreed Norgost. "But now the worst. Tell them the worst, Vegglestrom."

Caireen sat down. She had been going to give the gnomes a row for stealing, but they were so sad she realized they were not to blame. But she frowned, because stealing really was wrong. Especially for *Santa's* gnomes.

"Everything is now wrong," said Vegglestrom. "We are afraid of being caught going into people's houseses. Last night, Norgost and I tried to cheer ourselves up with a game of tennis with our old snow shoes for rackets, and your mother's tennis balls – we will give them back —"

"That's all right," said Caireen.

"Oh, we will."

"It's all right."

"We vill."

"No, please…"

"Ve will."

"Tell us the worst!" hissed Edward.

"The worst!" said Vegglestrom. "Oh, the worst! Vell, the vorst is this! Ve do not get enough to eat, so ve be too veak to work full steam ahead. Ve do not have the stuffs to make the doys even if we do be steamed up with food – "

"But what does that mean?" gasped Caireen.

Edward stared very hard at Vegglestrom, and Caireen wanted to sit close to Edward and pat his curls again.

"It means," said Vegglestrom with tears in his wrinkles, "that this December…" He rubbed his woolly sleeve up his cheeks. "It means," he whispered sadly, "that this December, there vont be no Christmas."

NOT
A GOOD IDEA

"How we dream," whispered Vegglestrom, after a long sad silence, "of the Summertime Santa. I can see Father Christmas now, striding around the North Pole in the cold bright sunshine, laughing his jolly *Ho! Ho! Ho!* Oh, Norgost, will we ever hear it again?"

Norgost's head was shaking while Vegglestrom spoke, and it shook more at his question, in great wide sweeps, sending tears flying from his cheeks, wetting the woolly mountains.

"Watch out!" said Edward wiping his face. "I washed already this morning. But I do wish you weren't so unhappy. Perhaps we can help."

"Yes," said Caireen, who had been thinking of crying to keep the gnomes company, but had decided to keep her tears for later. "Edward is good at solving puzzles. Perhaps he can think of something really clever."

She looked at Edward who frowned wisely, and the gnomes dabbed their wrinkles with their sleeves and tried to smile but only – really – became more wrinkly.

"Maybe," said Edward – and the gnomes stared at him hopefully – "I could teach you a cheerful song instead of your sad one."

"Oh," sighed Vegglestrom.

"Oh, horribles," said Norgost.

"Perhaps that's not a good idea," admitted Edward.

"Maybe," said Edward – and the gnomes stared at him hopefully – "I could bring you vegetables from our garden, instead of the worst quality scone mix."

"Oh," sighed Vegglestrom.

"We would have to cook them," said Norgost, "and Mother Christmas would know, and we'd have to tell her ve have spoken to you."

"Perhaps that's not a good idea," admitted Edward.

The gnomes sagged where they sat, cheeks drooping.

"Maybe," said Edward – and the gnomes stared at him hopefully – "I could send Father Christmas a THANK YOU letter."

"Oh," sighed Vegglestrom.

"He would know it came from just next door," said Norgost, "and guess ve have spoken to you."

"Perhaps that's not a good idea," admitted Edward.

Caireen couldn't think of anything, so she sat amid the socky mountains listening to the *whirr! whirr!* of the knitting machine and the murmur of Mother Christmas as she talked to the person who had come in from the hall.

Suddenly, the murmur stopped. Caireen
listened, shushing Edward who was making
another suggestion. Footsteps shook the floor,
and the gnomes shrank against each other in
horror.

"Only Santa – " cried Norgost – "can
tremble the floor through all the layers of
socks! He is coming this vay! You must hide!
Hide! Never in all times has a human child
seen Santa Claus! Hide, childrens, hide!
Hide!"

CHRISTMAS IS CANCELLED!

Caireen hid where the gnomes had tried to hide. Headfirst into the socky mountain she dived, wool rough on her face, woolly smells in her nose. She hoped she wouldn't sneeze. She felt Edward burrowing beside her. Strong hands (belonging to Norgost or Vegglestrom) gripped her feet and pushed, heaving her into the dark, warm nest.

Even in the depths of the mountain she could feel the floor tremble under Santa's feet.

The trembling stopped, very close.

"Ho," said a deep, sad voice. "Vegglestrom and Norgost. Not working?"

Caireen imagined the gnomes shaking their heads hopelessly.

"It doesn't matter, derribly," said Santa. (A thrill chilled Caireen as she snuggled safe beside Edward – Santa Claus was speaking almost close enough for her to touch! Oh, how silly she had been not to believe!)

"Look at these letters," said Santa. "I thought – for one moment I thought they were THANK YOU letters – then I opened them, and vot are they, Norgost? Vot are they Vegglestrom? I will tell you. Oh, they *are* from children. Listen to the first letter.

> DEAR SANTA, I WANT A BICYCLE FOR
> CHRISTMAS. I DON'T REALLY
> BELIEVE IN YOU, BUT DADDY
> SAID I HAD TO WRITE THIS LETTER
> OR I WOULDN'T GET NOTHING.

"And the second letter," moaned Santa.

> DEAR SANTA, I WANT LOTS OF NEW
> CLOTHES. I WANT THAT GREAT
> DOLLY IN VOOLVORTH'S VINDOW.
> PLEASE DON'T BRING ANY APPLES.

"And the third letter," groaned Santa.

> DEAR SANTA, I VANT A PICNIC
> HAMPER AND A MILLION SWEETS
> AND A BIGGER BAIR OF DROUSERS.

"Do you believe the selfishness?" asked
Santa. "Every letter begins, I WANT. Can you
believe this first letter saying she doesn't
believe in me, yet she asks for a bicycle? I
don't believe it.

"Is there no child in this world who ain't
greedy? I have come to tell you, Norgost –
and you Vegglestrom – vot I have decided.
These letters – " Santa's voice rose and a tear
bubbled in his throat – " have decided for me.
There is no point in going on —"

"But Santa!" cried Norgost and
Vegglestrom.

"No point. I am about to tell the other
gnomes. I have discussed it with Mother
Christmas. She says I must do vot I think
best. It is cancelled. This year, for the first
time in ages, Christmas is cancelled. Oh,
dear."

SOBS
SQUEEZING

Silence sat with Caireen and Edward inside the woolly mountain.

Caireen began to think that Santa and the gnomes had left.

She was about to nudge Edward to make him wriggle from their hiding place, when a sob squeezed up from somebody's insides.

Then another sob squeezed up from somebody else's insides.

Then another sob squeezed up – a long way – from somebody else's larger insides.

Caireen thought a sob was thinking of squeezing up from *her* insides, but she decided to keep it for later. Though it *was* awful that Santa should be so unhappy, just because children were thoughtless.

Caireen wondered if Edward had written a

THANK YOU letter to Santa after last Christmas.

Then she remembered that *she* hadn't.

Caireen felt dreadful. This is partly my fault, she thought. Imagine *no Christmas* just because of me! I didn't write because I was beginning to think Santa wasn't real! Oh, how awful!

"And now," said Santa's voice, "I am putting on my blue suit, and to the Job Centre I am going."

"The Job Centre!" cried Norgost's voice. "But you are Santa Claus! Father Christmas cannot get a job! And vot vill ve gnomes do? And wot do ve do with all these mountains of socks and stockings!"

"Burn them," sighed Santa. "Take them into the garden and have a bonfire."

"Burn them!?"

"Mother Christmas was making them into gnome clothes, yes? So what good are gnome clothes when you be looking for a job also?"

"A job also?" gasped Vegglestrom and

Norgost.

"Tidy up the jeans and jumpers you borrowed when you were out stealing socks and stockings," said Santa. "You don't want peoples staring at you."

"Santa! Santa!" cried Vegglestrom. "I am four hundred and twenty-two years and eight months of age! Norgost is three years older! How can ve get a job!"

"Think how old I am," said Santa wearily.

"And vot!" cried Norgost desperately, "do ve do with the doys ve stole to fill the boxes?"

"I don't care no more," sighed Santa. "Do vot you like. Burn them."

Caireen felt the floor shake as Santa tramped away.

She wriggled from the mountain and tumbled out amid a flurry of socks and stockings. Edward rolled beside her.

Vegglestrom and Norgost stood staring at nothing, their wrinkles deep with misery, tears dripping onto the woolly floor.

"It be the end of everything," sobbed Vegglestrom.

"The end," snuffled Norgost. "Think how peoples vill be behaving when there is no Christmas to remind them of kindness."

"Is there nothing we can do?" asked Caireen. "Edward, can't you think of something?"

Edward shook his head.

"Then it really is the end of Christmas," whispered Caireen, and the tears she had been saving for later, and the sob she had been saving for later, were just what she needed.

She sobbed, and let out the tears.

WE CAN'T LET CHRISTMAS END!

"We might as well go home," said Edward.

"Thank you for trying to help," whimpered Norgost.

"You are kind and indelligent children," sighed Vegglestrom.

"The knitting machine isn't saying *whirr whirr*," remarked Caireen, as she followed Edward and the gnomes to the door.

"She will be pudding it in its box and returning it to the shop where she stole it," groaned Norgost.

Caireen *really was* shocked at this, but her heart sat too sad inside her chest for her to speak.

She trudged behind Edward and the gnomes into the hall.

Once we leave this house, thought Caireen,

there will be no one to change Santa Claus's mind. It *really will* be the end of all Christmases.

She trailed after Edward and the gnomes along the passage towards the kitchen.

"People will be *so disappointed*."

Caireen dragged herself behind Edward and the gnomes through the kitchen.

"There must be *something* we can do."

Caireen slouched after Edward and the gnomes, into the little room beyond the kitchen.

Vegglestrom opened the back door.

The trees stared in from across the lawn.

"Goodbye," whispered Vegglestrom.

"Boodguy," whispered Norgost.

"Goodbye," whispered Edward.

"Goodbye," whispered Caireen.

Vegglestrom held the door.

Norgost stood aside.

Caireen imagined Mother Christmas sneaking into the shop to return the knitting machine she had stolen.

How awful for dear Mother Christmas!

How awful for dear Santa Claus!

How awful for the dear gnomes!

How awful for everyone if there was no Christmas just because she and Edward walked out of this house!

"I'm not going!" whispered Caireen. "Edward you've got to DO SOMETHING! WE CAN'T JUST LET CHRISTMAS END!!!"

PUSHING CLOTHES

Vegglestrom shrugged.

Norgost said, "Oh, how ve dream of the Summertime Santa! Do you remember, Vegglestrom, only last July, all us gnomes hammering and sewing in our workshops at the North Pole, and Santa vould stride in, fat and jolly in his red suit —"

"Hold on," said Edward.

"You've got an idea?" asked Caireen eagerly.

"Well," said Edward, "I don't know how to save Christmas..."

"Oh," said Caireen.

"But I know how we can get time to think."

"Oh!" said Caireen.

"Santa said he'd put on his blue suit to go to the Job Centre —"

"Yes?"

"What if he can't find it?"

"He wouldn't be able to go to the Job Centre, and we would have time to think!" gasped Caireen.

"It's no use," sighed Norgost. "He vill be bulling on his drousers at this minute."

"No, he won't," said Edward. "He was going to tell the other gnomes about Christmas being cancelled."

"He vill still be speaking in the upstairs sidding room," said Vegglestrom, "where we gnomes are pudding doys in boxes! But," added the gnome sadly, "will you really think up an idea to save Christmas?"

"How do I know!" shouted Edward. "But Caireen is right! We can't just walk away! Come on you two! Show us where Santa keeps his suit!"

Edward and Caireen pushed the gnomes back through the kitchen, and the gnomes hushed Edward and Caireen.

Edward and Caireen hurried the gnomes

along the passage, and the gnomes led them tip-toeing into the hall and up a staircase, listening outside a door to Santa's mournful voice and the stillness of the other gnomes.

"This is it," said Vegglestrom turning the handle of another door. "Santa's bedroom."

They huddled in and stood in the middle of the room.

Caireen reached out and touched Santa's bed. She had actually been in the same room as Father Christmas (the room with the socks and stockings), now her fingers were touching his real! real! quilt!

Though if we don't do something, thought Caireen, Santa will be just another man in a blue suit looking for a job!

"The wardrobe," said Edward. He opened the large old wardrobe's door and peered left, inside. Caireen peered right inside.

"I see a blue suit!" she whispered.

"Someone is coming up the stairs!" hissed Vegglestrom.

"It's Mother Christmas!" gasped Norgost.

"I hear the rustle of her skirt!"

"Get into the wardrobe," ordered Edward.

Caireen knelt up onto the wardrobe's floor and shuffled her knees among red suits with white furry trim, red nightgowns, and Mother Christmas's red dresses.

A strong hand scraped behind Caireen, and she grasped it and hauled in Norgost. Edward pulled up Vegglestrom.

They scuffled, untangling arms and legs, pushing hanging clothes to make space for their faces.

They stayed still as the bedroom door creaked, and footsteps walked across the carpet.

The only other sound Caireen heard was a teensy scratching like someone sharpening a pencil.

Which stopped.

SANTA
SUBBOSES SO

Caireen kept quiet. Edward, Vegglestrom and Norgost kept quiet.

Caireen heard a noise like knees bumping onto the carpet. Caireen thought Mother Christmas was kneeling to reach under the bed. Then a hollow cardboardy sound came into the wardrobe, like a box-for-a-knitting-machine sliding. Then Caireen heard puffing, and the bed groaned as if Mother Christmas had leaned on it, to stand herself up.

Caireen knew that Edward was rather good at thinking.

She didn't know *how* good until...

The hanging clothes swung, whispering quietly.

The whisper came closer to Caireen as she sat snug in the wardrobe's darkness.

She felt the warmth of Norgost's breath on her ear. Norgost whispered, *"Edward says to move to his side of the wardrobe."*

This seemed extremely risky to Caireen. She could still hear Mother Christmas and the cardboard box, but she did what Edward said, following Norgost in a silent slither across the wardrobe's floor, hoping the coat hangers wouldn't jangle, until she was jammed tight with Edward and the gnomes.

Whatever was Edward thinking about? wondered Caireen.

Then she heard deep gnomy voices sobbing as the gnomes left the sitting room, and the tramp of Santa's feet came into the bedroom.

"Are you really going to the Job Centre, dear?" asked Mother Christmas.

"Nothing else to do," sighed Santa.

"Shall I lay out your blue suit?"

"I subbose so."

"You've done your best, dear."

"I subbose so."

"It's not your fault children are so selfish."

"I subbose not."

"It's time you had a change." Mother Christmas's voice approached the wardrobe. "Perhaps you're too old for climbing inside chimneys."

"I could do it for another two thousand years," groaned Santa, "if there was any point."

The wardrobe door clicked.

Caireen crouched, squeezed close as a sandwich, against the gnomes and Edward.

Now she knew why Edward had told her to move to his end of the wardrobe. Santa's blue suit was at the other end.

Hangers jangled, and the clothes swung.

"Here it is, dear," said Mother Christmas's voice, and Caireen glimpsed the tail of the blue suit whisking into the daylight. Then the wardrobe door shut.

If Caireen had dared, she would have said, "*Very* good, Edward!" She smiled instead to the darkness. Then her smile slipped.

Her heart beat fast.

How silly she was!

Because she'd been smiling at Edward's cleverness, she had forgotten why she was in Santa's bedroom – to hide his blue suit!

Mother Christmas had given the suit to Santa!

In a few minutes he would be walking to the Job Centre!

FUNNY-LOOKING
MOTH HOLES

"You slip out of that dreary black tunic, dear," said Mother Christmas. "That's it. Give me those trousers. My, they are dirty. You've been wearing them since you changed out of your red ones, last July. And you moved house in them. Get into your blue suit, and I'll pop this black lot in the tub."

Caireen heard Mother Christmas walk out.

She heard the sort of sounds her dad made when he was struggling into clothes he hadn't worn for a long time, and knew that Santa was putting on the blue suit.

Oh, dear, thought Caireen. Is there nothing we can do?

Then Mother Christmas's voice came puffing up the stairs, saying, "Oh, dear! Oh, the poor gnomes! They are so upset. I'll be glad to see the last of those socks and stockings though, I can tell you!"

Then she came into the room and said, "Turn round, Santa, dear, till I look at you. That blue suit's a bit tight. What's this down the back of your sleeve? Come nearer the window so's I can see. Moth holes? I thought moths knew better than to go into Father Christmas's wardrobe!

"Turn round again. I declare! There are holes all over the back of your jacket!"

"And in the knees of the drousers," said Santa as if he didn't care.

"Funny looking moth holes," said Mother Christmas. "More like someone's been sticking a pencil through your suit."

"Nobody vould do that," sighed Santa.

"Someone has. Look for yourself."

"I don't care."

"Well, I do! You can't go to the Job Centre like that!"

"Vot does it madder? Nobody's going to give a job to a two-thousand-year-old chimney sveep. That's all I am."

"That's not all you are! Not! Not! Not! Who else in the whole world has spread happiness for so long? How dare you say bad things about yourself! Remember you are my husband! And nobody says bad things about my husband! Not even you!"

Feet thumped to the wardrobe. The door leapt open. Caireen's heart clumped about inside her chest. *Jangle!* cried the hangers. The clothes danced angrily, and Caireen glimpsed the tail of a red tunic whisking into the daylight.

"Put that on!" ordered Mother Christmas. "Put it on," she said gently. "And I'll put the kettle on. I've been keeping a bit of last year's Christmas cake – just for you."

Mother Christmas left.

Caireen listened to silence.

A gnome's leg pushed out from the tangle of legs and arms in the wardrobe, and a sigh touched her ear. Caireen hoped they would not have to stay crushed up much longer.

She heard the sound of a blue jacket dropping on the carpet. Then the sound of blue trousers. Then the sound of red trousers and a red tunic being put on. She thought she heard the sound of a broad belt, black as liquorice, being buckled around a fat tummy.

She heard Santa say, "Hmm," as if he was pleased with seeing himself in a mirror. Then footsteps left the room and the door closed.

EDWARD
GIVES ORDERS

Groans filled the wardrobe.

Elbows creaked and feet scraped. Caireen opened the wardrobe door and fell out onto the carpet. The gnomes and Edward fell out on top of her.

"The holes in Santa's suit," gasped Norgost, "be good luck, eh?"

"I don't think so," said Caireen.

"Of course it be good!" said Vegglestrom.

"Yes, it be good, all right," said Caireen, "but it wasn't luck. Was it Edward?"

"I used your pencil," said Edward. "The one you slipped on when we came into this house. Sharpened it with my pocket knife. I didn't like damaging Santa's suit."

Caireen was slightly sad that one of her grandad's pencils had been sharpened after so many years of being flat at both ends, but she was glad that Santa was not on his way to the Job Centre.

She went to the window, while Edward – who had been in the furthest corner of the wardrobe and very crushed – got his legs straight.

Below Caireen, in the garden, a huge pile of socks and stockings was walking across the lawn.

"Edward."

The pile of socks and stockings fell onto the grass, leaving a panting gnome (who had been carrying the socks and stockings).

"What?"

"The gnomes are building the bonfire."

Edward came to the window.

"Can't you think of something?" asked Caireen.

"They vill be taking out the toys soon," said Norgost at Caireen's elbow.

"And our many, many boxes," sighed Vegglestrom.

"*Will* they?" said Edward, and Caireen looked hard at him. Was there an idea in Edward's head?

Edward turned to Norgost and Vegglestrom. "You must help the other gnomes," said Edward.

"Help them?"

"Help them," said Edward, "and make sure the toys are in a separate pile from the socks and stockings. Burn the socks and stockings first!"

"First?"

"Go on!" cried Edward.

"Please do it!" urged Caireen.

The gnomes urged each other through the door, and Caireen stared at Edward. She reached out and patted his red curls.

"Don't do that!" said Edward. "We must get home," he told Caireen. "Quickly. And here's what you do. Telephone everybody you know. Get them to telephone everybody they know. And get *them* to telephone everybody *they* know."

"But what for?"

"Tell them there's a huge bonfire in your next-door neighbours' garden, and that toys are being given away free! Everybody is invited!"

"But what good will that do!" cried Caireen.

"You'll see," said Edward.

"Will *you* be telephoning everybody you know?"

"Yes," said Edward. "And everybody I don't know. Follow me."

Caireen followed Edward to the bedroom door. Edward peeked out, listening.

"There's someone down below in the hall!" said Edward. "Hurry!"

"We must hide here!" gasped Caireen pulling Edward back into the bedroom.

"It may be Father Christmas!" hissed Edward. "He'll come in here and we'll be trapped!"

Edward peeked out, listening again. "Someone's coming up the stairs! Come on!" He darted towards the sitting-room door which the gnomes had left open.

He looked back at Caireen and waved at her to follow, but she hesitated, wondering if she should hide again in the wardrobe.

Edward beckoned fiercely.

Caireen took one step out of the bedroom. Too late —

THANK YOU
VERY MUCH!

A large hand appeared from below, gripping the banister. Silvery curls bobbed up the stairs, and shoulders in a red tunic.

Caireen opened her mouth in a silent scream. *Nobody should ever see Santa Claus!*

She ran to the wardrobe.

Santa's footsteps bumped up the stairs.

The handle of the wardrobe door rattled in Caireen's grasp. She said, "Eeeeek!" very quietly.

The footsteps thumped towards the bedroom.

There was no time to climb into the wardrobe and shut the door.

Caireen looked round.

There was no time to scuttle under the bed.

Only one hiding place was left – and it

wasn't a good one.

The door handle rattled.

Caireen ran silently across the carpet.

The door opened, and she stepped between the curtain and the window.

She didn't even dare look at her feet to see if her toes were hidden.

She breathed through her mouth so as to make no noise.

She heard a sigh. The bed creaked as if Santa had sat on it.

Santa sighed again.

Silence.

Then Caireen almost ran out from her hiding place. She heard a sob. Not the mournful sort of sob the gnomes had made, but a sob that had no hope in it. A sob that felt that life had no purpose.

"No burbose," sighed Santa to himself. "No one cares enough to say THANK YOU to old Father Christmas. Even my blue suit lets me down. Moths should know better. I never had moths before in my suits. They should have eaten this red tunic. I ain't got no use for red this Christmas. I can't even go to the Job Centre – not dressed up like Santa Claus. I am Santa Claus. I forgot. It seems like summertime since I was really Santa Claus. Never vill I be Santa Claus again. Though I enjoyed my liddle bid of Christmas cake." Sigh.

"Vot a long day this has been. It is getting dark."

The bed creaked and footsteps approached the window.

It really was quite dark. Caireen hadn't noticed.

And, at first, she didn't notice a red flicker of light on the curtains. Her heart was using her stomach as a trampoline.

Father Christmas was staring out the window *right beside her!* The red flicker brightened, and Caireen turned her head slowly, to look outside.

Father Christmas was so dismal he didn't see Caireen.

A mountain of all the socks and stockings danced in flames.

The fire shone its light on another mountain – a mountain of stolen toys packed in boxes, ready to be given out for a Christmas which wouldn't come.

Unless Edward's idea works, thought Caireen. Whatever it is.

She noticed Santa leaning forward to peer into the dusky garden. Caireen looked and saw Edward striding across the lawn.

He must have run down the stairs after

Father Christmas came into the bedroom.

Behind Edward walked a boy. Behind the boy walked two girls. Behind the girls walked more boys. Behind the boys walked more girls.

More boys ran onto the grass and watched the bonfire.

Dozens of girls flooded the lawn and talked around the bonfire.

Scores of children poured into the garden chatting and giggling.

Father Christmas leaned on the windowsill and stared.

"Vot are they doings?" he muttered. "All these ungrateful childrens! Vot do they vant in my garden?"

"Listen!" Edward's voice floated up to Caireen. He was talking to the boys and girls.

"Listen!" said Edward. "Do be quiet! I told you there are free toys. And here they are. In these boxes. Help yourselves! *But don't go away!*"

The children surged towards the pile of boxes. Voices rose excitedly to Caireen. Father Christmas stared until it seemed his eyes would fall out.

He said, "They are taking the toys! They are daking my boxes! I didn't give them permission! Oh, children are so greedy! I am glad Christmas is finished! I am glad! I AM GLAD!!!"

He swung away from the window and thundered across the room. The bed crashed as Santa threw himself down.

Caireen wondered what Edward's idea was. Surely he didn't just want to give the toys to the children. Surely —

Caireen missed what Edward was saying now, because the bedroom door opened and Mother Christmas came in and spoke gently to her husband, saying, "Don't be angry with them, Santa, dear. They're just children. I saw them from the kitchen window. They're doing no harm. I know they seem ungrateful, but... What's that they're saying?"

Caireen, too, wondered what the children were saying. She had been busy listening to Mother Christmas.

The children were speaking again, all together, and Edward was standing before them waving his arms like a conductor with an orchestra.

"Thank you very much," said the children.

"Did you hear that?" said Mother Christmas.

"No," said Father Christmas. "It doesn't matter vot they say. Tell them to go home."

"Thank you very much!" said the children.

"I think they said, 'Thank you very

much!'" said Mother Christmas.

"They can't have!" grumbled Father Christmas. "They don't know how." But the bed creaked and two pairs of footsteps crossed the carpet.

"Thank you very much! Thank you very much!" shouted the children. "THANK YOU VERY MUCH! THANK YOU VERY MUCH!"

"They *are* saying THANK YOU!" whispered Mother Christmas.

"I hear them!" gasped Father Christmas.

"THANK YOU VERY MUCH!" yelled the children.

"It's almost as good as Christmas!" shouted Edward. "But not quite! THANK YOU VERY MUCH! THANK YOU VERY MUCH!"

Father Christmas's arm was around his wife's shoulders. She waved to the children in the garden – though in the gloom of evening Caireen knew the children could hardly see her. Father Christmas's hand reached up and touched the glass. He waved.

The children waved back.

"THANK YOU!" came scattering up from the garden. The children began to leave.

"THANK YOU!"

The bonfire of socks and stockings burned up quickly sending shadows and red light among the trees.

The pile of toys had gone.

The last child beckoned towards the window.

It was Edward.

Caireen slipped from behind the curtain. Father and Mother Christmas were too wrapped up in each other's arms to notice.

Caireen tip-toed to the door.

"Enough," she heard Mother Christmas say.

"Enough," agreed Father Christmas. "We be behind in our work this season. Vot a silly old fool I am being. Feeling sorry for myself instead of thinking of the childrens. Get rid of that vorst quality scone mix and those old loaves. I think there be enough money in this suit pocket to buy decent grub for our gnome friends. And flours for you to bake with. And mincemeat for the Christmas pies. And a few new tools. And I vill phone the removal van so we can get home to the North Pole…"

Caireen walked quietly down the stairs and out into the garden.

She smiled at Edward and he smiled back. He gave her a plastic pencil case full of her grandad's pencils. "I found them in the toy pile," he said.

Caireen and Edward looked up at the bedroom window and called, "Thank you!"

Two hands waved behind the glass.

"Thank you!" called Mother Christmas.

"Thank you!" called Father Christmas.

"Thank you very much!
MERRY CHRISTMAS WHEN IT COMES!"